DATE DUE

~~Beege 11-97~~	Kaur		
T-74	NOV 20		
11-98	Patty		
~~11-98~~	~~Ross~~		
11-1-99	Mendy		
	NOV 19		
RJF	NOV 22		
M-76	DEC 4		
DM7	NOV 26		
SR10	NOV 29		
~~JS11~~	~~DEC 2~~ NOV 27		
S. Lei			

$11.00

A TURKEY FOR THANKSGIVING

A TURKEY FOR THANKSGIVING

by Eve Bunting

Illustrated by Diane deGroat

Clarion Books

New York

Clarion Books
a Houghton Mifflin Company imprint
Text copyright © 1991 by Eve Bunting
Illustrations copyright © 1991 by Daine de Groat

Library of Congress Cataloging-in-Publication Data

Bunting, Eve, 1928–
A turkey for Thanksgiving / by Eve Bunting ; illustrated by Diane
de Groat.
p. cm.
Summary: Mr. and Mrs. Moose try to invite a turkey to their
Thanksgiving feast.
ISBN 0-89919-793-0   PA ISBN 0-395-74212-9
[1. Thanksgiving Day—Fiction. 2. Turkeys—Fiction. 3. Moose—Fiction.]
I. de Groat, Diane, ill. II. Title. PZ7.B91527Tu 1991   [E]—dc20
90-21871   CIP   AC

Watercolors were used to create the full-color artwork.
The typeface is 12 pt. Galliard.

WOZ 10 9 8 7 6

To Glenn, who insists on a turkey for Thanksgiving.
—E.B.

To Florence, and the memory of Thanksgivings past.
—D.D.

It was Thanksgiving morning. Mr. Moose helped
Mrs. Moose set the Thanksgiving table.

"Sheep will sit here. He likes a chair that's straight
up and down," Mr. Moose said. "Rabbit here.
Porcupine here. Mr. and Mrs. Goat here." He smiled
at his wife. "Isn't it nice to have friends to share
Thanksgiving?"

Mrs. Moose set two paper pilgrims, one at each end of the table. She placed the paper turkey with its great fan of a tail between the candles, and stood back.

"They look good, my dear," Mr. Moose said.

Mrs. Moose sighed. "Yes. But I wish we had a real turkey. Everyone always has a turkey for Thanksgiving. Everyone but us."

Mr. Moose nuzzled Mrs. Moose's head. "Well, that won't do. I will go this minute and find you a turkey for Thanksgiving."

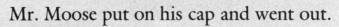

Mr. Moose put on his cap and went out.

Mist wandered through the bare trees. The cold made his nose water.

Rabbit poked his head from his rabbit hole. "Mr. Moose! Is it dinnertime?"

"Not quite yet. Mrs. Moose wants a turkey. I'm off to find one."

Rabbit joined him in three quick hops. "I'll come, too."

Moose's warm breath hung white in front of him. Snow crunched under his hooves and made little holes that Rabbit jumped over.

"I see the Goats," Rabbit said.

Mr. Goat raised his head and spat out the tin can he was chewing. "Is it dinnertime?" he called.

"Not till I find a turkey," Mr. Moose said.

"We saw one down by the river," Mrs. Goat told him, and Mr. Goat added, "A fat one."

The Goats leaped down from their perch. "We'll show you."

Sheep was farther up the hillside, looking round as a fur ball in his winter coat. "Is it dinnertime?" he bellowed.

"First I have to find a turkey," Mr. Moose bellowed back.

"There's a turkey nest on the riverbank," Sheep called. "Wait for me."

The earth smelled of ice and moss as they crunched along. Above them a crow hung, black as a puff of wood smoke.

Porcupine was hiding in the underbrush.

"It's you," he said and put his quills down.

"We're off to get a turkey for Mrs. Moose," Mr. Moose explained. "Do you want to come?"

"I'm slow," Porcupine said. "Pick me up on your way back."

"Who'd want to pick you up?" Sheep asked, and laughed his bleat of a laugh.

"I'll wait," Porcupine told Mr. Moose.

They saw Turkey's nest right away, and Turkey
himself peering over the top of it.

"Turkey! Turkey!" Mr. Moose called in his sweetest
voice.

"Aagh!" Turkey blundered from his nest and ran.

Mr. Moose lumbered after him. "Turkey! Don't
run. We just want you for Thanksgiving dinner."

Turkey ran faster.

DO NOT DISTURB!
(come back after
Thanksgiving)

NO
Turkey
here!

Mr. Moose saw the red and blue sheen of Turkey's neck. Turkey's tail brushed crumbs of snow behind him as he tried to fly.

"Too fat," Mr. Goat said.

Turkey's legs bent in the middle as he fell.

Mr. Moose put a booted hoof on his head and smiled his great, toothy smile. "I hope you don't have other plans for Thanksgiving, Turkey."

He helped Turkey up. "My wife won't mind that you're too fat," he said. "Let's go. It's getting close to dinnertime."

They marched Turkey in front. "I'm sorry about this, for I can see you don't want to come," Mr. Moose said. "But I must insist. A promise is a promise."

There was a wreath of dried fruit on the Mooses' door. Inside, the house was filled with Thanksgiving smells. Mr. Moose hid Turkey behind him.

"Look who I brought, Mrs. Moose," he said. "Sheep, the Goats, Rabbit, and Porcupine. And ta-da!" He pushed Turkey around in front of him. "For you. A turkey for Thanksgiving!"

Mrs. Moose clapped her hooves. "I'm *so* happy to have you, Turkey. Thank you, Mr. Moose. Now everything's perfect."

"Shall we sit?" Sheep asked, heading for the straight-up-and-down chair.

"Let's." Mrs. Moose pointed. "Rabbit here.

Porcupine here. Mr. and Mrs. Goat here, and look!
I brought a chair from the other room in hopes
of Turkey."

"A…a *chair*?" Turkey stammered.

"Right next to me," Mrs. Moose said. "Light the
candles, Mr. Moose."

There were bowls of acorns and alfalfa sprouts, dried since summer. There was willow bark and cured grasses and wild parsley. There were pressed leaves, thin and pale as new ice on a pond.

"I hope you find something here to your liking, Mr. Turkey," Mrs. Moose said. "I wasn't sure of your taste."

"You are so kind to worry about my taste," Turkey said. "I thought you'd be worrying about *how* I'd taste."

"Heavens, no!" Mr. Moose smiled his big-toothed smile and filled everyone's cup with cold spring water. "It's so nice to have friends around the table at Thanksgiving."

Turkey's wattles wobbled. "It's even nicer to be AT your table and not ON it," he said. "Happy Thanksgiving, everybody."

"Happy Thanksgiving, Turkey."

Bank Street College of Education

People Read

Illustrated by Dan Dickas

THE MACMILLAN COMPANY, NEW YORK
COLLIER-MACMILLAN LIMITED, LONDON
COLLIER-MACMILLAN CANADA, LTD., TORONTO, ONTARIO

1-K

People Read

3

All over the city, people read.

People read on streets.

People read in stores.

People read in houses.

Boys and girls read in school.

All over the city, people read.

They read on streets and in stores.

They read in houses.

And they read in school.

All over the city, people read.

Good Morning

11

The sun.
The morning sun comes up.

12

Sunlight comes to streets and houses.
Sunlight comes to schools and stores.
Morning comes to the city.

13

People come out.

"Good morning," they say.

"Good morning."

Boys and girls come out.

"Hi," they say.

"Hi."

The boys and girls go up the street.

They go to school.

One boy runs.

He runs to school.

"Good morning, boys and girls."

Who Are They?

18

All day, people come and go.
Many people come and go.

In the morning, a man comes.

He comes up the street.

He goes to all the houses.

Who is he?
He is the mailman.

In the morning, a man comes.

He comes up the street.

He goes into a store.

22

Who is he?

He is the store man.

In the morning, a man comes.

He comes up the street.

He comes in a truck.

Who is he?

He is a workman.

At night, a man comes up the street.
He goes into a house.
Who is he?

He is the father.
"Hi," says the father.

Ann's Mother

Ann's mother goes to work.

She works at Ann's school.

Ann and her mother go to school.

Ann and her mother are at school.

Ann says, "Good-by, Mother."

"Good-by, Ann," says her mother.

"Have a good day."

Ann goes up to her room.

She reads and works all morning.

Ann's mother works all morning.
She works in the school.

The morning is over.

The boys and girls go to lunch.

They go down to the lunchroom.

Ann's mother is in the lunchroom!

"Hi," says Ann.

"Is the lunch good?"

"Yes," says Ann's mother.

"It is good."

34

Some Day

Some day I will have a truck.

People will stop.

Cars will stop.

I will say "Hi" to all the people.

Some day I will read many books.

I will read books at work.
Boys and girls will come in.
I will read to the girls and boys.

Some day I will have three boys.

People will come to see the boys.
The boys will say,

    "Hi."

       "Hi."

          "Hi."

Some day I will have a store.

I will have ice cream in the store.
People will stop.
They will come in.
They will all have ice cream.
And I will have ice cream.

Some day, some day!

43

Fire!

45

A man runs down the street.
"FIRE! FIRE!
A store is on fire!" he says.

Ee-ee-ee-ee-ee!

Cars and trucks stop.

People stop and look.

A fire truck comes down the street.

It is red.

Ee-ee-ee-ee-ee!

The street light turns red.

Cars and trucks stop.

The fire truck goes on!

The fire truck stops.
A red light on the truck turns.
It turns and turns and turns.

A fireman runs into the store.

Boys and girls run down the street.
"A fire!" they say.
"Come on!"

Some boys and girls run to the store.
They look in.

The fireman comes out.
A boy says, "Is the fire out?"
"Yes," says the fireman.
"The store man put it out."

The fireman is up on the truck.

The fire truck goes away.

The red light turns and turns.

A girl comes over to the store.
"Is the fire out?" she says.
"Yes," says a boy.
"The store man put it out."
"Some fire!" says the girl.

Ben and the Birds

Ben comes to see the birds.
The birds fly up.

The birds fly down.
They come to Ben.

Ben says, "Fly, birds."
The birds fly up.
They fly up high.
They fly away.

The birds fly over the city.

People look up at the sky.

"Look at the birds," they say.

59

The birds fly on.

They fly over streets and houses.

On and on, they fly.

Will they come back?

60

Yes.

The sun goes down.

The day is over.

The birds turn.

The birds fly back.

They come back to Ben.

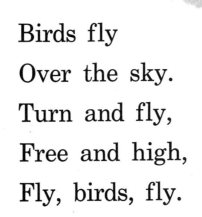

Birds fly
Over the sky.
Turn and fly,
Free and high,
Fly, birds, fly.

VOCABULARY LIST

People Read

People Read, the second Preprimer of the Bank Street Basal Reading Series, introduces 59 new words. The words marked with an asterisk are variant forms of previously presented words.

1. read	17.	31. room reads*	47. look
2.	18. who	32.	48. red turns trucks*
3.	19. day	33. lunch lunchroom	49. stops* fireman
4. all over	20. man goes a	34. yes it	50.
5.	21. is mailman	35. some	51. put
6.	22. into	36. I will	52. away
7.	23.		53.
8.	24. truck	37. stop cars	54. Ben birds
9.	25. workman	38. books	55.
10. morning	26. at	39.	56. fly
11.	27. father says	40.	57.
12. sun comes	28. Ann's mother	41. see	58. high
13. sunlight	29. she her Ann works*	42. store*	59. sky
14. come say		43. ice cream	60. back
15. Hi	30. good-by have	44.	61.
16. he boy* runs		45. fire	62.
		46.	63. free